SANDS

Love-themed contemporary fairytales,
illustrated poems & prose

Dr. Aashna Gill

ISBN- 9798482334997

Illustrations by Dr Aashna Gill and Gurseerat Kaur.

Cover design by postermywall.com.

Artwork by Canva and Pixabay.

To anyone who has ever appreciated my writing, thank you.

CONTENTS

All literary references are nerdy tributes.

TABLE OF CONTENTS

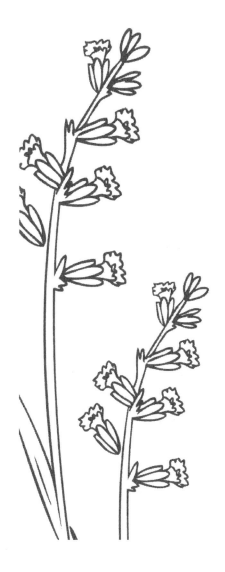

WHAT COULD BE

SERENDIPITY

Snow White[1], draped in a black and red saree, tiny golden earrings and pinned up shoulder-length hair, stepped into the sports bar with her guy friend. The after-party following the college function was already in motion, though with very few people and some forgotten faces.

Snow White and her friend spotted two of their batchmates at the reception area, so it was confirmed that the after-party was indeed happening. The maidens occupied the dance floor in sarees and the men in formals, all having come here after the college function.

Prince Charming[1] stepped in front and gave the two of them a warm welcome. He was dressed in a grey suit with a black shirt, tall, dark, and handsome. He greeted them both like they were his closest friends.

Few minutes there and *Snow White* concluded that the party was sponsored mainly by *Prince Charming,* who had given the college function a miss, yet here he was in his formals.

Charming escorted her, and they had drinks together. They had drinks together with others. Snow danced with her batchmates.

She sat on the couch with her friend while he head-bobbed to the music. She was enjoying herself thoroughly and smiling, seeing how well her DJ friend was engrossed in the music.

Several times *Charming* came up to *Snow*. They had conversations with him telling her about the recent happenings in his life, including a mail sent from the hostel authorities to vacate his room on account of substance abuse, holding a birthday party and making noise. They would talk, have a drink, and then lose each other in the crowd, not minding it one bit because of all the fun they were having.

While sitting on the couch with her friend, Snow watched *Charming* snugly slow dancing with a maiden friend of his who was too drunk. The hours went by. The fun never stopped. The next minute the maidens were all huddled in a car to go to the guys' flat to crash at for the night.

All the maidens were drunk senseless except for *Snow*, who could hold the same number of drinks as others but elegantly.

At the flat, the maidens were huddled into bed. The couples were in the hall, one in another room. Music played on, and soon everyone was dozing off.

Snow was hungry, and she mentioned it and was led to the kitchen by *Charming*. They sat on the shelf, and he started talking. They ate. People would pass in and out of the kitchen, yet their conversation continued. He again introduced her to the fresh faces as his good friend since his first year of college. This was their fourth year of college.

For five and a half hours, their conversation continued till it was seven-thirty in the morning.

AIR AND WATER

I am the air. He is the water. He welcomes me into him, and I gladly immerse in him. I am a bird naturally inclined to fly. He is the nest I need to return to because his heart is my favourite haven. He tends to build a wall around him, and I have the habit of coaxing him out of it. I take two steps back when I think he needs time on his own. Sometimes he takes the two steps forward to be with me again, much to my heart's delight. At times I am left there waiting, wondering if he will come around. But being two pieces of a soul, I walk the road back to him.

They say I leave him confused regarding how I feel about him and what I want from him. He inspires me to write. He inspires me to dream of my fairytale. Does that not say enough? I wish he were more expressive, but I am not sure that is what I want; because his silence and subtlety say more than any words could ever speak. I love him with all my heart. He is always on my mind. Does he feel the same?

LOVE AND OTHER THINGS

I found Love in a jar,

Fireflies surrounded by bars,

I am setting them free,

Just you, just me.

I found forgiveness in a smile,

In a bottle of beer in a short while,

In a dream a realisation,

My truth in hibernation.

I found my wings in honest talks,

In the earth spinning, in my long walks,

I found mischief in my wink,

Going over everything you think.

Let's follow every star,

Till we reach so far,

Where we skate on Saturn's rings,

Embracing Love and other things.

SIEVING THOUGHTS

Today I picked up my thoughts and sieved them,

Sat at the window plucking memories from the hem,

It's been three months since I put pencil to page,

Pour me a jug of words and watch my fingers race.

Idealistic daydreams come knocking at my mind,

Looking within myself, a loser, I find.

Take me to a land where kisses are slow,

Courage the currency, dreams in eyes glow,

And if you have to go away,

Slip me a cure, so the memories fade away.

TAKE MY HAND

Take my hand and let me take you away,

To a place so very far away,

Where you shall laugh, where you shall smile,

We'll walk together so many miles.

Let your voice surround my ears,

Let your presence fill my years,

Hold my hands and never leave,

Too full of Love, I can barely breathe.

THE WIND BENEATH MY SAILS

Here and there, in a breeze faring near,

Your thought comes sailing and is welcome here,

I am caught smiling in a pirate's gear,

Carry me out of bed was a risky text, dear.

We could be vagabonds or members of a cluster;

I'd follow happily, blinded by your lustre.

You are my cup of coffee after an accomplishing day,

Fuzzy feeling, long talks, let's drive away.

ECLIPSE

The first raindrop on you,

Vividness of nature around you,

The perfect strength of coffee,

A love-flavoured toffee.

Take me to where the days are calm,

And my mind enveloped in a serenity balm.

My mind has fallen down a rabbit hole,

I could risk going through a K-hole.

SUNSHINE

I'll stay in your shadow coz you are my light,

Flickering and wavering, forever out of sight,

Snow-globes and mirrors, laughter and delight,

In your arms is my favourite place to hide,

I'll stay in your shadow coz you are my light,

Muffled smiles, naughty and nice, you are my knight.

A LITTLE SUNSHINE

All I want is a little sunshine,

A love so true it makes me smile,

A promise kept, a bond strong,

A relationship that lasts long.

You can give me your heart, and I'll keep it safe;

With my heart, you can have it replaced.

I can be the reason for your smile,

You can always stay by my side.

A love that needs no reason,

A love that lasts all seasons,

My tears on your palms when I cry,

My name on your lips when you die.

SOLO SONG

I talk to you, I think of you,

That is all I want to do,

To hear all that you speak,

And to wait till our hearts meet.

I chat with you about everything,

But not about what I think,

About you, about me,

About how perfect we could be.

I am scared you may say no,

I'd never want you to go.

In my heart, there is rain and rainbow,

And a song I sing solo.

My head is spinning,

So many feelings,

I lie here dreaming,

Plain wishful thinking.

Do you feel the same? I do not know,

Am I the one for you, would you know,

I will wait for you for eternity,

Till you realise I am part of your destiny.

IMPETUOUS

If I say I wrote for you,

How soon can I send it to you?

My Love is clumsy, awkward and abrupt,

How soon till you turn the temperature up?

Enquired and learned it could take a boy

seconds or a year to fall in Love.

I am way over the edge,

Haven't you waited for Love long enough?

Amongst the places in my heart, there is a home for you,

I have talked to the swifts,

I have talked to the winds,

To bring you home to me.

A ladybug promised to carry on a dandelion my wishing star,

to bring us close from a distance seeming far.

Miles and spaces and time no more

when flying lanterns reach the shore.

I have seen you in visions whilst high,

I have loved you in hushed voice whilst nigh.

I have sent you kisses on petals

and feelings in unrevealed letters.

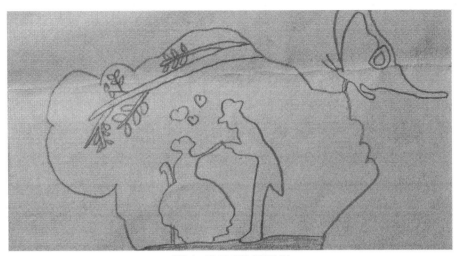

I'LL BE THERE

When you have no place to go, choose the road that brings you home;

When you have no one you know, walk towards the heartbeat you know.

When you need a place to hide,

I'll be there with open arms.

When the world feels a bad place,

Together we will clear the haze.

We can get through the nights,

Cuddled up near the firelight.

When all you want to do is drop,

I'll be there to make you strong.

When you find the end so near,

I'll be there to dispel all fear.

BOWS AND TIES

Winter nights, hanging from rails,

Clearest starry sky, moon in its best phase,

A call to a twin flame,

Love note sent to the same.

Can I line the stars for us?

Oblige me without a fuss?

Like a scent that can travel,

I am yours to unravel.

MY TRUE NORTH

Take this map and come to me,

Coz I know you feel the intensity,

Take this hammer and shatter the barriers,

Let loose all your inner terriers.

I'd click my heels and reach you

if you asked me to.

I would rearrange my life

if it meant being by your side.

WANDERLUST

Let's become hippy gipsies,

Or dive into deep seas.

I would rather be anywhere but here;

Installing a heart and soul in a robot was a doomed dare.

Let's envelop ourselves with music and books;

Before you enter, leave your formality on hooks.

Simple living, curious thinking, meaningful actions,

Meditation, green tea and organic rations.

Whisper into my ears all that stirs you alive,

I am looking neither for a nest nor a place to hide.

If kisses are your language, hugs are mine,

I do not belong to you, but my Love is thine.

PARALLEL WORLDS

Everyone needs love to magic their life,

Not a string of lovers who won't stay beside.

A chain of events to make you both see,

You are the one made for me,

With strength in hearts and patience unforeseen,

Let's make possible this beautiful dream.

Let's go to an antiques shop. I want something rich with history, something that survived.

I was told Love is nothing but a fairytale. I replied: I wouldn't want it any other way.

The concept of a fairytale is not finding the true prince but finding the true love.

DR AASHNA GILL

What Should Have Been

BREAK THE SPELL

"*Love is the closest thing we have to magic,*" thought *Snow,* rationalising her emotions. It had been two months since the all-morning conversation with Charming. She believed she had bottled the memory for a future glance through a *Pensieve*[1] . She had flowed every relevant detail about the preceding event. Describing the magic would make the *wisp* disappear.

EMPTINESS

There is an emptiness in my soul that begs release through words,

So I read you out, and I write you out.

You stick like tar to my soul,

And float like clouds above my head.

I rinse you out,

The bubbles play,

And I set it to another cycle again.

CINDERELLA'S SISTER

Like the glass slipper that did not fit,

Like the sister whose luck did not click,

I have been eyeing you since our eyes met,

The longed-for feast that I never fed.

We are the greatest Love that didn't happen,

The destined route never taken.

Hey Stranger, I have given it much thought;

Hence, in your arms, I am not.

I should have kissed you that morning,

But there is no spell for our Love's dawning.

All I have left of you are the words I wrote,

A parallel universe, a different us, hushed into a note.

LOVE NOTE

You can live in a memory for a lifetime,

2268 kilometres from who you call mine.

Cities we don't forget,

Paths for years we tread.

A love note to a city and its memories;

Strangers to share nostalgia with over pleasantries.

WHAT HAPPENED ?

What happened to all the dreams?

Beauties lying in deep sleep,

A kiss that woke them to life,

Princes who on white horses ride.

There are dragons everywhere,

Dungeons, dark alleys, despair,

Lamps that don't shine,

Chants that don't rhyme.

Challenges we no longer win,

A future that is dim,

What happened to courage leads to victory?

What happened to a happy, lively story?

PAST LAND

Meadows and Gates,

Pleasures at rates,

Gargoyles sneer at fallen angels,

Rangers no longer enjoy dangers,

Crooked minds behind perfect visages,

Heroes cowering behind rocks and hitches.

If a wizard could set this right,

You and I could be saviour and knight.

Wisps tell us to go back to sleep,

Because the swamp is thick and deep.

SAND SLIPS AWAY

Write your name in the sand, watch it get washed away,

Give someone your heart, watch him walk away.

Believe everything he said, and all you left unsaid,

Do you sometimes wish your heart was dead?

Would you live your life the way others want you to?

Would you stand up and be the real you?

Walk towards your dreams, walk towards you,

And now look around, how alone are you?

Is it wise to smile when things slip away?

Is it wise to watch and then walk away?

Is it wise to hold sand in hands, as they say,

Sand slips away; yes, it does slip away.

4 AM

Four in the morning, breeze in my hair,

Birds chirping somewhere near,

Walking on my balcony,

In a sleepless night spontaneity,

Music mixed with your thoughts plugged into my head,

Did you find someone as good as me in bed?

If time does not exist, I could wait forever,

Who's to say you will never get here!

Like the birds that chirp every morning,

A stubborn voice says our love is dawning.

PARK OF HUMANITY

Stroll into the park of humanity,

And tell me what you really see,

Smiles, happiness and joy everywhere,

Or hearts at breaking point of despair?

Does every word spoken have its meaning?

Is every promise meant for keeping?

Can you see behind the plastic smiles?

Can you see all those failed tries?

Do you think the one who's helping wants to?

Do you think the one who's laughing wants to?

Would you give your heart to be broken?

Would you give up your wings when shaken?

Walk out through the back doors, just go;

This is not the place for you, you know.

SURREAL REALITY

She looked in the mirror, the girl looked back;

It wasn't herself, that was the thought she had,

Before she could find an answer, she was caught in a dream,

So hazy and surreal, sometimes reality seemed.

She stepped onto a flowery, green meadow;

Another minute, it was just her and her shadow;

She looked at the sky, was that the sun or the moon?

How could she have grown up so soon?

She sat on the rock waiting for Love,

She wanted it soon, and soon enough,

She walked away before tears could hurt;

Now she has put a lock on her heart.

She shines so bright, disappears into the night,

A loner she is, but so full of life,

Don't walk towards her; she might push you away,

Keep your footsteps gentle, else she'll fly away.

QUANTUM ENTANGLEMENT

What if all I am is here in your arms?

What if all I am is far, far away?

Like particles, like energy, like electrons that are free,

Waves to the shore, crashing from the sea,

We meet each other yet I meet just me.

TEQUILA AND RUM

Two shades of brown- the eyes I remember vividly,

Tequila and Rum- what you do to my insides.

We catch each other's eye in the corridor, smile and walk on by,

You ask where I am running to,

Should say, "It's what I do."

I retraced my steps coz I saw you,

Walked back two steps to say you Hi,

You said you remember what I was wearing the first time you saw me,

You said I am funny and looked back at when we should have been friends,

You held my hand all morning, and there was nowhere else I'd rather be.

You are the heart-shaped kidney stone that moves every day to the mind, soul and body, leaving tremors in its wake. You are the holy committed sin. You are the strongest ecstasy dosage with a year-long crave.

Some days you are a shard of ice entrenched in my heart.

I lived a lifetime in those hours.

You looked at me like you could save me, and I looked at you like you could.

People chafe us like sandpaper. They burn us down like candles when all we did was care. We were born into the world to add more love and care. Anyone who brought change to the world did not accomplish it with anything less.

It's a grave mistake to build shrines in our heart for people who don't deserve mementoes.

Sometimes I read the stories I wrote to confirm to myself that it was all true, every single detail.

WHAT IT IS

Ariel[2] , the mermaid, sat on a large rock in the ocean from which the shore was visible. Her fellow ocean beings flapped around. Dolphins were lolling near the surface, and a school of red puffer fish floated just below the surface. The ocean bed bustled with its majestic corals home to sea horses and crabs and giant pearls in their oyster shells.

Every once in a while, *Ariel*'s guiding star granted her legs to venture into the world of humans. Once in a blue moon, she would feel a connection with a man.

Later, in the ocean, she would replay the event in her mind. She would crush on the person. Some would find their way into her words.

Yet no one pursued her. The connection ended with the event, or as she liked to hope, continued in their minds. She desired a huge romantic gesture made by someone she felt an emotional connection with.

MEETING THE NEW PERSON

Uneasiness finds her, vying for her attention. She knows Uneasiness will not leave her till Uneasiness has poured out her heart to her. Procrastination defends her against Uneasiness. She knows he is a protective friend.

Some delays cannot be delayed. Some changes are best faced. She welcomes Uneasiness into a rich wooden room lined with shelves of books, the titles of which she doesn't acknowledge with a glance. Near the fireplace, they sit in comfortable armchairs. The knowing look of Uneasiness gives her a shudder, and she pulls up her shawl.

Yes, she is ready for the heart-to-heart conversation. Her life will have to wait. She looks into the ornate mirror. She is not who she was a few days back. Life has a clever way of changing every belief you have. There are a hundred steps between the now and then, and like a dutiful traveller, she has walked each one of them.

Uneasiness talks with her about the recent events that changed her into this new person. Together they build a new perspective on life. She acknowledges who she is, and together they walk towards a distant heaven.

POTLUCK

Can you be free, or are you free and needlessly bind yourself to people and things? Love, a gem that has held fascination since the beginning of time. What teaches us companionship also teaches us to return to our individuality. What makes us bless others also leaks out the wrath of karma on people we shed tears for.

How hopeless is the human heart! How unreasonable it is! Like a child fixated on an animal it wants as a pet, the heart keeps running to that on which it has stamped its love, despite rejections.

I could see in you a million faces and none of them remotely pretty. Yet if the moon was offered to me on a platter, I would choose your multiple personalities.

"Ghosts talking to us all the time- but we think their voices are our own thoughts."–David Foster Wallace.

The few times that [3]*Emma Swan* opened the door to her emotions, she had this uneasy feeling that she had walked into the wrong play and was now expected to play the protagonist. For a woman who found delight in music with meaningful lyrics, she was expected to thump to shrill white noise. The anguish in her soul was bursting from the seams. There were too many people in this world- those jabbering creatures with an aura of negativity that they wanted to throw upon you.

UNLUCKY IN LOVE

What do you do after you have exhausted all words? What is the plausible action after you have sent him your writings about him in a momentary impulse? There are pores in my heart that sometimes coalesce into a large hole. What am I supposed to say I feel when most times I have to gulp art to feel something?

We are our own demons, and nothing he will say or do or not say or not do because that too is an action, can quieten the demon that shouts, *"All I have loved I have loved alone."*

HOW YOU BECOME A GOOD WITCH

You are born one. As your hormones kick in and your energies surge, it overwhelms you. At thirty, you start to draw energetic boundaries when you see your health and academics derailed by lack thereof. It's a cycle of embodying your power and giving it away.

QUASARS[5]

It's been three years, still living in your shadow,

Have always knighted you with Order of the Halo.

Quasars[5] polarised on the same axes,

In the cosmic web with limited access.

Crystal balls and fated happenstances,

Touch, go and ever-solo trances.

MUSE

We are pieces in a puzzle,

Looking for the other.

You are the hop to my step,

The rugged in my bed,

My hottest fantasy,

You are the sweetest delicacy,

I am the name on your lips,

You are the reason for my bliss,

You are the truth I refuse,

My all-time muse.

SAND IN HANDS

I'm looking at the shore,

The one I've been swimming to,

Finally, the dream has come true.

I look at the horizon,

Nothing's different, no omen to guide too,

The water's not clear the way it's supposed to.

I look at my reflection,

I have choices to make,

Decisions to take.

I hold the sand in my hands,

The dream of a young heart,

But the stone in my head is hard.

Faces surround me, known, unknown,

Some ask me to hold tight my dream,

Some ask me to let it be.

I watch the confusion, my mind's blank.

Whatever I decide, I can't just walk back.

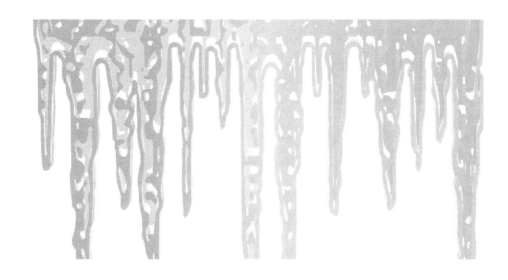

ICICLE

A sliver of ice, a burst of cloud,

A decaying heart, a black shroud.

Time and again, tasting a bloody wart,

Releasing a hundred birds from this caged heart.

Close your eyes, change the locks, lose the keys,

Words were never meant to be messengers, how deceitful this seems,

Blatant honesty is the sleepless nights and the howling screams.

I lit a candle for you in my heart, then fanned the flame,

The guide never reached you but set me aflame.

I wrote a note, clenched my teeth on it,

Heard my bones break; this is not how it started.

From chasing butterflies to searching for a dragon's egg,

The quest consumed me; drowning is what I dread.

I am bleeding words from unknown wounds,

Yet you sit there, such a pretty face, for which I mooned.

NYCTOPHILIA

Some nights we count sheep jumping over a fence,

Some nights we talk all night with friends,

Nights are young, days a blur,

Look at that celeb- you are better than her,

Coz you got substance and brains,

And freedom to run in the rains.

What's open till two, where you can eat at four,

Is knowledge privy to us, we know so much more.

You, me, a dog and beach,

Hands close enough to reach,

Sands beneath, stars above,

Mythology and Constellations- you could learn from us.

SLEEPLESS

When lullabies can't put me to sleep,

When your picture in my mind repeats,

I count the stars, I gaze at the moon,

I hum a song from dawn to noon.

When you enter my talks,

When you invade my thoughts,

There is a smile on my lips,

A reason for my bliss.

THE STORY OF A LITTLE FAIRY

This is the story of a little fairy,

A beautiful story, but a little scary.

She was born to a couple not very far,

The man said he was blessed by the higher power.

She was the joy in the sadness,

The calm in the madness.

She would take the man's tears and blow them away,

She would stand by the man when the world walked away.

One day, an evil, dark sorcerer walked by,

How could he stand so much joy!

He played with the mind of the man,

He had his wish; he destroyed the clan.

The little fairy and the man now hold back tears,

No one takes the first step; each has his fears.

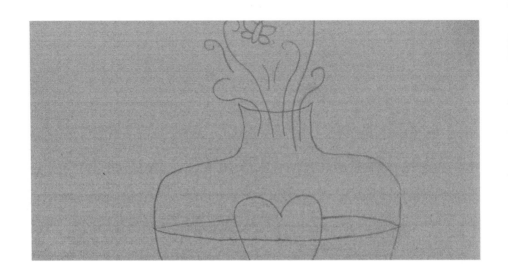

CHASING THE SAME HIGH

I am still locked in your energy,

Still smitten by your frame,

I am still craving our synergy,

Still loading the saved game,

Zorbing our memory,

Orbiting our history,

Chasing the same high,

Picturing You and I.

THE GREAT HALL

Both walked into the hall in cloaks shaded purple,

Minds a myriad of thoughts,Egos that refused to humble,

She was the first to break,

The first to negotiate,

Witnessed by the indifferent,the fabricator, and the

facade.

LET THE ADVENTURE BEGIN

You love me,

I saw a fog lifted,

Your stony visage melted,

For a split second my derailed self found it's track,

For a moment I held the world in my hand.

Stopping time with kisses,

Touch and tease and misses.

The world in a room,

A room with the world,

Vibrant and glittery,

Each taste a savoury,

Smiles and laughter,

And adventure hereafter.

Give me all the colours on a palette,

And let me splash those on a duvet.

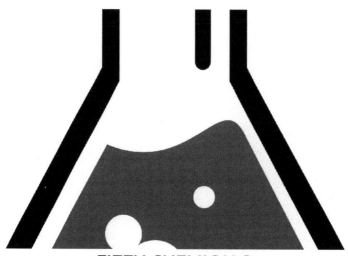

FIZZY CHEMICALS

Here I am listening to songs you asked me to,

Here I am doing nothing new,

Just wanting to be near you.

Peacocks in fields, drives, full moon, the breeze,

The whooping, the talks, the comfort, the ease,

Out of rhythm, in tune to the heart,

On a hillside boldly sharing our art.

We are young and reckless,

Emotional or couldn't care less,

Wisest sages near low tide,

Most powerful witches at Yuletide.

I keep you hidden in bookmarks and highlighted texts,

Consulting oracles for us, for what happens next.

I wrote you a letter and slipped it into the void,

I put all the love hearts in a jar,

Sealed the lid with a kiss to not set it ajar.

The happiness that radiated on your face on seeing me,

The shivers I feel when you telepathy.

I have been looking for a moment with you,

All my life, with all my soul,

My name on your lips has me believing you want more.

I took a gulp of air, sighed heavily,

Remembering the night I couldn't breathe coz of ecstasy.

METEORITE

Never seen a star as bright as you,

Never felt an intense heart break

akin to a blossomed flower's petals separate.

Two sentences from your lips

are two weeks' ecstasy as day drips.

The breath that escapes me,

that moment I am not me.

Anxiety, forgetting to breathe,

transformed into pleasure when you meet.

Give it time and space,

Destiny is a kitten playing chase,

Unraveling the yarn,

Too slow, too fast, darn.

It's a ball out here, each asking for a dance,

The maidens kissing the frog, giving it another chance.

Heavenly fires won't rain,

Mantras to ward the pain.

LOSING ALL

I'm losing all I thought was mine,

The sanity, the smile, the perfect life.

The laughter, the beautiful lie,

They hear as they see me die.

I don't feel anything at all,

Slowly walking towards where I fall.

At the edge of the cliff, and I have no wings,

I can clearly hear the doom bell ring.

SOUL TO SELL

I try to smile,

My heart is breaking inside.

I fake a laugh,

I've had enough.

I watch the world pass me by with joy,

There's no way out; my heart's a broken toy.

My shadow is not dark enough to hide me,

In the limelight-not where I want to be.

I watch the birds fly in the sky,

I wish to be there up high,

Bound with chains, tortured in hell;

For a moment of peace, I'd give my soul to sell.

DEEP WATERS

Like logs of wood floating in the river,

Like untrained swimmers in icy water quiver,

Like the sun plunging into the sea,

Am I a part or the world a part of me?

Deep waters, blue sea,

Who is me?

Storms, waves or streams,

Nightmares or fulfilled dreams?

The reflection is clear,

The future is near,

Touch the surface,

And you'll see it disappear.

SCRIPT

There are questions without answers,

Reasons we don't go after,

Feelings we don't embrace,

Dreams we delay to chase.

Alone in my quiet moments,

I'm haunted by my presence,

The shadow or the soul,

A part or the whole.

Life has a script, so they say,

In it my part, I gladly play,

The background score turns into noise,

Dance to the tune, no other choice.

The mind plays its tricks,

The heart foolishly clicks,

A wave, smile, a wishful sigh,

Returns with a tear in eye.

THIS IS MY LIFE

Shadows and silence, light and noise,

Rainbows and rain, wild and poise,

No retakes, no flashbacks,

No critics can hold me back.

Secure in sweet love,

Friendships to hold me up,

I jump into puddles and slip too bad,

But what is life if no fun you had?

Laughter and tears,

Hugs from dears,

Incessant talks,

Silent walks.

This is my life,

I'm trying to get it right,

Aims and dreams to walk the mile,

Courage and Love and a perpetual smile.

STAINS

Take a picture and burn it,

Embers then ashes,

Dig out a memory and enslave it,

Then madness dashes.

Light then dark, dark then light,

The heart doesn't know wrong from right,

Silence or Words, Strandedness or Flight,

Nothing kills the conflict inside.

Let go of balloons, drive by the moon,

Why was the end sudden and so very soon?

Wisps that only I see, Emotions that only I feel,

Be still, dear heart; you make my head reel.

STATUE

I stopped making shrines to men,

Lighting incense at altars for them.

I stopped reaching out in concern,

Treading on coal paths making me burn.

I look out from my window,

In rare moments on go,

I sit with myself,

Living on self-help.

UNREAD

I write like I breathe,

Unsteady, forgotten wheeze.

I write our saga,

Interrupted drama.

I write you into existence,

How I woo you with persistence.

Writer's block hits

Each time you slip.

You have been the ink to my pen,

My ruin among men,

A snatched glory,

A tragic story.

CAPITOL

A windy, sunny day; coffee gone cold,

In the busyness of life, a story left untold.

In the snow, in a beachy town,

A destiny cycle coming around.

Blazing music and chirrups,

And unwarranted hiccoughs.

Wings flapping hard, feet unground,

Flags dividing the world, hearts safe and sound.

A sleepless night, a lukewarm tea,

A million thoughts rushing through me,

The pouring sky, the parched earth,

The breeze, moments I can't breathe,

The ancient temple, the hopeful prayer,

A promised visit when you are here.

Under the same sky, we share the same earth,

In a parallel time, the rain from the same hearth.

All my thoughts carried by breeze,

Rumble from the sky, return to tease,

Flashes and flashes like memory lapses,

Roaringly lower timeline collapses,

A singular sound, a bell in the collective mind,

Asking each of us what did we find?

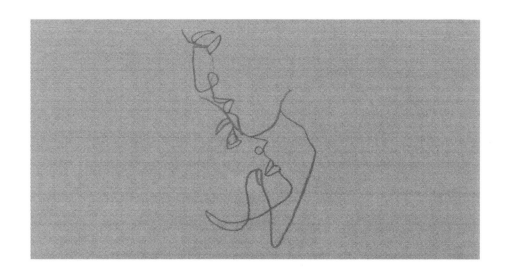

LOVERS IN DREAMS

Lovers in dreams are kinder,

Even chance of a peaceful asunder.

My heart is in its rightful place,

Beating in our calm embrace.

Lovers in dreams are mine,

A moment caught out of time.

CITY LIGHTS

City lights and a bustling road

in a city far away

But her mind is on a different road.

How responsible are we for another's life?

How guilt-tripped are we for another's plight!

I see airplanes taking off from roads,

I hear so many people's woes,

No one is where they want to be,

Would you trade with me your misery?

Beacons of light fading in the distance

like a lighthouse

or the anguish of sirens?

I see auras screaming for help,

Tough to silence my soul's whelp.

It takes a lifetime to learn how to live,

It takes a lived life to regret it all.

I fade into open spaces,

Hopelessly chasing artificial lights.

If you meet fireflies, won't you tell them to come find me?

Oh well, let it be because every moment, I burn and flicker.

I fly away to nowhere,

Seeing constellations in shards of glass.

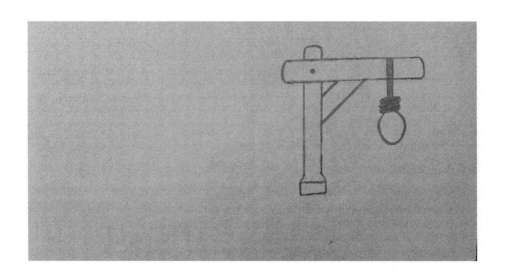

DEATHSMAN

They called your name and led you to the gallows,

They smeared your name from angels with halos.

You are stuck in the in-between,

At how good it did once seem.

"Pull the noose," you scream,

"Sever the head from the heart,

Cut the constant thought stream."

HOODED

You look like a man back from war,

One who has seen hell and all,

Weary footsteps, silence to numb the explosion,

This time no faked cruelty to muffle the implosion.

You are vulnerability standing near the door,

Saying goodbye when you want to be stopped once more.

CONFESSIONS

Here I am in these lonely hours in this desolate place,

where nothing happens or not often enough.

It pains from head to toe,

My soul has nowhere to go.

In the dark, I am reminded of a forgotten path.

Wounds don't heal the way they used to.

I resort to old, wrong patterns,

Coz the world I can't fathom.

I taste deceit on my lips,

while I gulp bitter, health drinks.

I chose this path, and I chose logic,

But here my heart is empty,

and tears brim my eyes.

I am not fine,

I haven't been fine for a very long time.

PROMISE

Watch the sun split into an array

of colours of love I gave away.

Drink yourself into darkness

till you take home your madness.

As you begin another stoned day,

Regret you left,

I promised I'd stay.

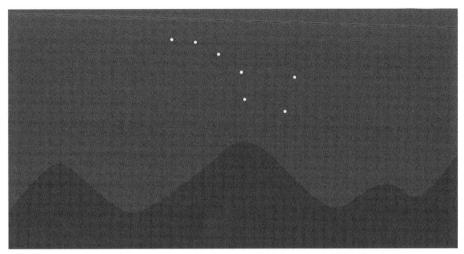

STORIES OF CONSTELLATIONS
AND LASSES BENEATH THEM

My words are an echo in the void,

Sound of a glass shatter from the toit.

Hallowed be the name of thy Love,

Hallowed the turf she walks on,

Tinted the window I gaze thee from,

Heavy the sighs I gulp on.

Tick-tock the clock ticks by,

Fragrance of Love that chimes by,

A sound stuck in my throat,

Memory playing a learned note,

Veils and action brazen,

Harp Of Vega carried to Heaven.

TALES OF THE SEA

Ships sailing towards the lighthouse,

Sailors looking for innkeepers that may house.

The Captain thinking of the journey,

Not the heart he left on the gurney.

Sirens drowning wretched sailors,

Revenging a love that wavered.

YOU MAKE ME BELIEVE IN LOVE

All my life I've been running,

Heartbreaks around me leave me dreading,

Of the thing they call Love,

And all the lovey-dovey stuff.

When you look at me with those beautiful eyes,

There's a rainbow in my heart and a sunrise,

The fear ebbs and hope lights up,

I journey to the sky higher up.

You make me believe in Love,

And that the world is good enough.

You make me believe in Love,

You make me believe in our love story.

The times when I feel I am lonely,

You appear from the clouds just for me.

The times when I need to hear you speak,

You surround me with your voice and make life sweet.

You make me believe in Love,

And that the world is good enough.

You make me believe in Love,

You make me believe in our love story.

MY BEST DREAM

I woke up from sleep on a call from you,

Eight years it had been, and you appeared out of blue.

Something clicked the way nothing else did,

You talked for hours about us as kids.

I smiled when you talked about girls,

I laughed at the way your mind worked.

We could talk for hours, the way we did,

Honest and nice, two perfect misfits.

I was a dreamer, and you were my dream come true,

You opened my eyes to a fairy tale so new.

All your little secrets I hold in my heart,

The words you spoke fasten the beat of my heart.

You were my best dream I said goodbye to for reality,

We were meant to be, but I gave up to destiny.

I am an enigma; you are an afterglow,

Unravelling hastily for a one-person show,

Exchanging lucks with kisses,

Such soothing embraces,

More pleasure than I can bear,

Hug so tight I gasp into your ear,

The longing and yearning keep the energy alive,

When our paths merge, it's a symphony live.

COMETS

If all I am is here, then why my core is merged with you?

If reality is what it is, then why in dreams do I see you?

Millions on the planet, hundreds we cross paths with,

A stroke of destiny for us to have found this,

We make each other come more alive,

No longer can I settle for a lesser life.

Are words the measure of emotions?

I am surprised to find you in rotations,

I dip my nib in an ocean,

The only colour it soaks is your lotion.

Like comets hurtling through the sky,

Each a rock till we make fire.

SUGAR

Sugar, you sound like a melancholic song,

Played on record all night long.

Your soul's crazed on the surface,

Comparing your grace to her face.

It's been a long, lonely journey,

With knaves in a tiresome tourney,

The quest for a loving, brave knight,

Ended with your sword lost in the fight.

KALEIDOSCOPE

Since we parted, I have held a kaleidoscope,

It has a tube that goes from future to the past,

Mirrors reflecting logic in the events,

Glass coloured by miraculous moments,

When I look into one end of the tube and turn it,

I am overwhelmed by the changing patterns of emotions.

I built an art museum to us,

Abstract though it may sound, I kept us analogous,

I trail my fingers on the calligraphy,

And chiaroscuro with charcoal on canvas.

I put us on a façade just to view foreshortening,

Then I prayed at the altar and let the door open.

Monsters lurk entwined to the souls of those you love. Some will stay with the monster instead of you.

Dr Jekyll and Hyde,

Behind masks, some demons hide.

Behind Beast is a wonderful man,

That's a lie only *Disney* sang.

Judge or Suffer,

Society is a danger.

Lock your heart and bury it in a safe place,

The search for a soulmate is a dangerous maze.

SPARKS

In a world full of confetti,

Of people travelling to Haiti,

I found bliss in a book,

Comfort in my favourite nook.

Surrendering to a man's charms,

Dreaming of loving arms,

Nail-biting anxiety,

Actions of reckless variety.

I found the moon too small,

DR AASHNA GILL

Lassoed it to an auk,

The moon dipped in the sea,

And I laughed heartily.

Sparks flew from my fingers,

Destroying everything that hinders,

Electrified the earth,

Flowers rose from the berth.

FAIRY-DUST

Walk through the doors of the troubled present,

The sun's in line to greet, but first, it's the stars and the moon crescent.

A miracle is riding its way to you,

Through roadblocks, flat tires and some delays,

Eventually, it will reach you and kiss you awake.

The future is a bright place,

Filled with candies, adventures and multicoloured palette.

Everything is possible, all wishes come true,

You reflect on your broken dreams, not seeing the opportunities new,

Sprinkle yourself with fairy dust,

Life is beautiful; move forward, you must.

I will kiss you when the sun goes down,

Hold your hand when you feel alone,

Show you the glittering stars at night,

Reel in magic to make everything right,

I could kiss your tears,

Spell away your fears,

Just say the word, I am right here.

There is a yearning in my heart that can't be refused,

A desperate plea that can't be noosed,

It knocks and knocks and whimpers too,

Moonlit howls, letters with vervain dew.

CALL ME BY YOUR NAME

Call me by your name,

so I can be certain

you feel the same.

Call me when I run through your head

like the finest whiskey

strongest at best.

Call me by your name

when we lie naked,

and I gaze adoringly your frame.

Universes collapse and are created when we embrace.

I keep hugging a cactus believing it will transform into flowers.

We are not flames that died. We are perfume dispersed in the air.

I left a lover in that city, a lover that never came looking for me.

A writer's words are like a spider's web. Reality and imagination are intricately woven.

Sometimes the worst failure paves the path for the best success.

I understand the fascination with snow globes. It is about having a living memory suspended out of time.

Maybe we write to throw a match on our gasolined self.

I want you to remember me like the softest prayer on your lips.

Sometimes I think that if you cut me, you will find words and emotions flowing through my veins.

Your name escapes me like a prayer.

Till you haven't dealt with the past, you can't walk into the future.

SILENCE IS PEACE

"What is this life if full of care?

We have no time to stand and stare."

Our brain works very fast, at the rate of a thousand thoughts at a time. How would it feel to shut it down for a while? With no past, no future, not even the present, just the moment and what it offers. No asking why, not even how, just accepting and being at peace with the universe and with ourselves.

Not figuring out what we should do in the coming years, not looking down on ourselves for having failed, just knowing we are exactly where we should be and safe in God's love.

Life is a chain of events. Everything has led us to where we are now, and what we are going through now will take us somewhere beautiful. Instead of the hundred doubts about life, why not trust it as our best friend?

Who says there is no magic? I have captured you in words, and there we shall always remain.

I say goodbyes with every breath.

A piece of my past will always stay buried in the words I wrote.

SEED

THE DESCENT INTO MADNESS

On the train home, I chatted up my fellow passenger,

And listened to the story of this interesting Stranger,

What I learned I have nothing to show for it,

Except a warning bell in my mind to normalize shit,

Such is the frailty of human spirit,

Metastasing autophagy by mind to best of it,

Don't end up in a looney bin,

No matter how loud your mind din,

This may be a small measure for success,

But enough for someone who only knows excess.

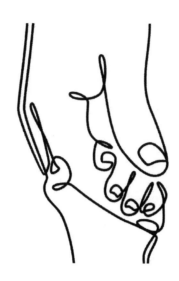

DEAR GRANDAD

The little signs, the silent voice,

All that you do,

To let me know you are here.

I believe in angels,

Coz I have you,

I believe in God,

Coz you taught me to.

Would never have known Love,

If not for you,

Would never have known me,

If not for you.

The hands I held that taught me to walk,

The words that boosted me to the top,

The friend I have always had,

I love you, dear Grandad.

You never know how much capable you are until you are inspired or challenged.

Sometimes the worst failure paves the path for the best success.

Till you haven't dealt with the past, you can't walk into the future.

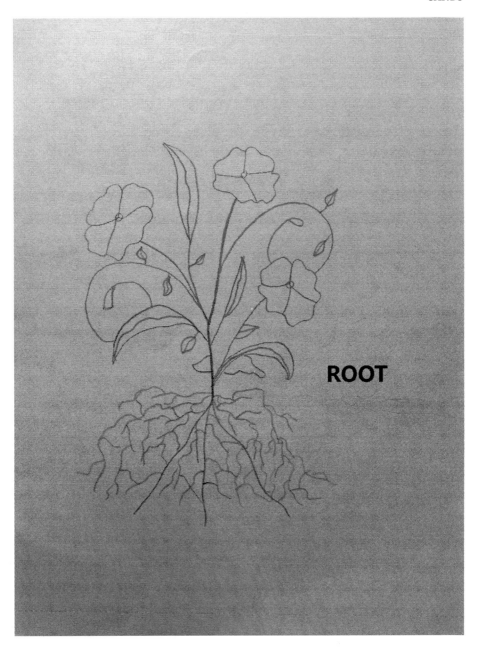

ROOT

ROOTS

How it came back to me! I was back in the school church, and it was twenty years ago. I could hear the choir singing hymns and see my ten-year old self screaming Hallelulajah with her best friend. The wonderful surprise of the occasional selection to attend Sunday morning mass. The rare privilege to be seated in the gallery above, the eagle's view of the altar proceedings and the gossip about only the Christian teachers being offered wine. The bustle of maroon uniforms with white veils. Special breakfast.

SHOOTING STAR

In search of a shooting star, I walk here, I walk there,

In hope of a second chance, I look everywhere.

I'd like to say I don't give a damn to the world,

But the truth is I do care about what they say.

I don't want to stand alone in the dark,

I don't want my world to fall apart.

My world is beginning to crumble, or is it in my mind?

Is my blanket of loneliness a trick of my mind?

There is a new beginning, there is a new dawn,

Somehow the past doesn't let me move on.

I walk two steps forward, the past catches up with me,

I grin at him confidently because I trust in me.

BUD

HOW TO BREATHE

Thirty years and I still forget how to breathe,

Still haven't learned how to drop asleep,

My thoughts could put a bullet train to shame,

A genius mind stammering its own name,

So many masks, so many selves,

And only cannabis helps.

THE FALLEN WARRIOR

This is the story of a mighty great warrior,

He was a winner and always a victor.

Battles he won, recognition he had,

He believed his strength to be in the sword in hand.

The mighty warrior had a fall,

Lost his sword and his soul.

From the zenith of glory, he fell to the abyss of humiliation,

He roamed his kingdom with no self-realisation.

After years of wandering, he found the answer he sought,

He was the sword, not the sword his strength.

A pauper he had become,

Decided to get back his kingdom.

He lost battles again and again,

Till one fine day he made it plain,

He won the battle, his kingdom, himself,

It took some time, but he proved himself.

Just when you finish achieving one dream, there's another dream waiting to be achieved.

And then it rained, and all that was dirt was swept away from her soul.

[1]*Snow White* and *Prince Charming*: names used for no other purpose than to define the protagonist's character: charm.

[2]*Pensieve*: where my fellow *Harry Potter* fans at?

[3]*Ariel*: Disney character, the quintessential mermaid.

[4]*Emma Swan*: *Once Upon A Time* television series' character

[5]Quasars: astronomy.

ABOUT THE AUTHOR

Dr. Aashna Gill

Born in Amritsar.
Studied at Sacred Heart School,
Dalhousie.
Started writing poetry at the age
of thirteen.
Has won prizes for her English
and Hindi writings.
Bachelor of Dental Surgery from
Manipal University,Mangalore.
Master of Dental Surgery Conser-
vative Dentistry & Endodontics.
This is her second book which so

far has ranked as 7th bestseller on Amazon Australia & UK and as
49th bestseller on Amazon India.

BOOKS BY THIS AUTHOR

Ashes

The book 'Ashes' consists of emotional, inspiring and motivational poems. It also comprises a love story, few other stories and thought-provoking prose.

Printed in Poland
by Amazon Fulfillment
Poland Sp. z o.o., Wrocław
05 May 2022